Sarah Morgan Bryan Piatt

Dramatic Persons and Moods

Sarah Morgan Bryan Piatt

Dramatic Persons and Moods

ISBN/EAN: 9783337334369

Printed in Europe, USA, Canada, Australia, Japan

Cover: Foto ©Andreas Hilbeck / pixelio.de

More available books at **www.hansebooks.com**

DRAMATIC

PERSONS AND MOODS,

WITH

OTHER NEW POEMS.

BY

MRS. S.º M. B. PIATT.

BOSTON:

HOUGHTON, OSGOOD AND COMPANY.

The Riverside Press, Cambridge.

1880.

RIVERSIDE, CAMBRIDGE:
STEREOTYPED AND PRINTED BY
H. O. HOUGHTON AND COMPANY.

CONTENTS.

———•———

DRAMATIC PERSONS AND MOODS.

CONTENTS.

WITH CHILDREN.

DRAMATIC PERSONS AND MOODS.

DRAMATIC PERSONS AND MOODS.

REPROOF TO A ROSE.

Sad rose, foolish rose,
    Fading on the floor,
Will he love you while he knows
    There are many more
    At the very door?

Sad rose, foolish rose,
    One among the rest:
Each is lovely — each that blows;
    It must be confest
    None is loveliest.

Sad rose, foolish rose,
    Had you known to wait,

And with dead leaves or with snows
 Come alone and late —
 Sweet had been your fate !

Sad rose, foolish rose,
 If no other grew
In the wide world, I suppose
 My own lover, too,
 Would love — only you !

TWO IN TWO WORLDS.

A PEASANT girl sat in the grass,
  With just a peasant's eyes to see
The king's fair son when he should pass; —
  From farthest Fairyland was he!

" He cannot love me — but he might,
  If this or that had chanced to be.
It breaks my heart to know how slight
  The things that hold him high from me.

" Had I been born in yonder tower,
  With just a jewel for my hair, —
Not half so sweet as this one flower, —
  He would have climbed to reach me there.

" Just for some fairness in my face,
  Some ermine on a train of state,
Some poor, dead name that he could trace
  To royal tombs — I were his mate!

11

" So brief the distance then between
    Palace and hut, need I be sad ? —
Almost he loves me. Ay, a queen
    I were — if but a crown I had !

" Ah me, unhappy in my place !
    What matter, since they are apart,
Whether one rose-leaf or all space
    Divide divided heart and heart ? "

  . . . . . It was a thousand years ago.
    To-night Time tells the tale anew :
I am that peasant girl, I know ;
    And, sir, the king's fair son are you !

12

WHY, sir, as to that —— I did not know it was time for
  the moon to rise,
  (So, the longest day of them all can end, if we will
  have patience with it.)
One woman can hardly care, I think, to remember an-
  other one's eyes,
  And —— the bats are beginning to flit.
  . . . . We hate one another? It may be true.
  What else do you teach us to do?
  Yea, verily, to love you.

My lords — and gentlemen — are you sure that after
  we love quite all
  There is in your noble selves to be loved, no time
  on our hands will remain?
Why, an hour a day were enough for this. We may
  watch the wild leaves fall
  On the graves you forget. . . . . It is plain
  That you were not pleased when she said —— Just
  so ;

Still, what do we want, after all, you know,
But room for a rose to grow?

You leave us the baby to kiss, perhaps ; the bird in
　　the cage to sing ;
　The flower on the window, the fire on the hearth (and
　　the fires in the heart) to tend.
When the wandering hand that would reach some-
　　where has become the Slave of the Ring,
　You give us — an image to mend ;
　Then shut with a careless smile, the door —
　(There 's dew or frost on the path before ;)
　We are safe inside.　What more ?

If the baby should moan, or the bird sit hushed, or the
　　flower fade out — what then ?
　Ah ? the old, old feud of mistress and maid would be
　　left though the sun went out ?
You can number the stars and call them by names, and,
　　as men, you can wring from men
　The world — for they own it, no doubt.
　We, not being eagles, are doves ?　Why, yes,
　We must hide in the leaves, I guess,
　And coo down our loneliness.

14

God meant us for saints? Yes — in Heaven. Well, I,
    for one, am content
  To trust Him through darkness and space to the end
    — if an end there shall be ;
But, as to His meanings, I fancy I never knew quite
    what He meant.
  And —— why, what were you saying to me
  Of the saints — or *that* saint ? It is late ;
  The lilies look weird by the gate.
  . . . . Ah, sir, as to that — we will wait.

THE DESCENT OF THE ANGEL.

" THIS is the house.   Come, take the keys,
  Romance and Travel here must end."
Out of the clouds, not quite at ease,
  I saw the pretty bride descend ; —
With satin sandals, fit alone
To glide in air, she touched the stone.

A thing to fade through wedding lace,
  From silk and scents, with priest and ring,
Floated across that earthly place
  Where life must be an earthly thing.
An earthly voice was in her ears,
Her eyes awoke to earthly tears.

16

HER WORD OF REPROACH.

WE must not quarrel, whatever we do;
   For if I was (but I was not!) wrong,
Here are the tears for it, here are the tears: —
   What else has a woman to offer you?
Love might not last for a thousand years,
   You know, though the stars should rise so long.

Oh you, you talk in a man's great way! —
   So, love would last though the stars should fall?
Why, yes. If it last to the grave, indeed,   .
   After the grave last on it may.
But — in the grave? Will its dust take heed
   Of anything sweet — or the sweetest of all?

Ah, death is nothing! It may be so.
   Yet, granting at least that death is death
(Pray look at the rose, and hear the bird),
   Whatever it is — we must die to know!
Sometime we may long to say one word
   Together — and find we have no breath.

   2   17

Ah me, how divine you are growing again ! —
   How coldly sure that the Heavens are sure,
Whither too lightly you always fly
   To hide from the passion of human pain.
Come, grieve that the Earth is not secure,
   For this one night — and forget the sky !

18

A WOMAN'S PROMISE.

Enough I love you, after years and years,
To write Love in your grave-dust with my tears.
And after you whom shall I love? At most
Only, ah me, a dead man — or a ghost!

19

CAPRICE AT HOME.

No, I will not say good-by —
  Not good-by, nor anything.
He is gone. . . . . I wonder why
  Lilacs are not sweet this spring.
  How that tiresome bird will sing!

I might follow him and say
  Just that he forgot to kiss
Baby, when he went away.
  Everything I want I miss.
  Oh, a precious world is this!

. . . . What if night came and not he?
  Something might mislead his feet.
Does the moon rise late?   Ah me!
  There are things that he might meet.
  Now the rain begins to beat:

So it will be dark.   The bell? —
  Some one some one loves is dead.
Were it he —— !   I cannot tell
  Half the fretful words I said,
  Half the fretful tears I shed.

Dead?   And but to think of death ! —
  Men might bring him through the gate :
Lips that have not any breath,
  Eyes that stare —— And I must wait !
  Is it time, or is it late ?

I was wrong, and wrong, and wrong ;
  I will tell him, oh, be sure !
If the heavens are builded strong,
  Love shall therein be secure ;
  Love like mine shall there endure.

. . . . Listen, listen — that is he !
  I 'll not speak to him, I say.
If he choose to say to me,
  " I was all to blame to-day ;
  Sweet, forgive me," why — I may !

A GHOST AT THE OPERA.

It was, I think, the Lover of the play:
  He, from stage-incantations, turned his head,
And one remembered motion shook away
  The whole mock fairyland and raised the dead.

I, in an instant, saw the scenery change.
  Old trees before me by enchantment grew.
Late roses shivered, beautiful and strange.
  One red geranium scented all the dew.

A sudden comet flung its awful vail
  Around the frightened stars.   A sudden light
Stood, moon-shaped, in the East.   A sudden wail
  From troubled music smote the spectral night.

Then blue sweet shadows fell from flower-like eyes,
  And purplish darkness drooped on careless hair,
And lips most lovely — ah, what empty sighs,
  Breathed to the air, for something less than air !

22

Oh, beauty such as no man ever wore
   In this wan world outside of Eden's shine,
Save he who vanished from the sun before
   Youth learned that youth itself was not divine!

I might have touched that fair and real ghost,
   He laughed so lightly, looked so bright and brave —
So all unlike that thin and wavering host
   Who walk unquiet from the quiet grave.

Myself another ghost as vain and young,
   And nearer Heaven than now by years and years,
My heart, like some quick bird of morning, sung
   On fluttering wings above all dust and tears.

But some great lightning made a long red glare :
   Black-plumed and brigand-like I saw him stand —
What ghastly sights, what noises in the air !
   How sharp the sword seemed in his lifted hand !

He looked at me across the fading field.
   The South was in his blood, his soul, his face.
Imperious despair, too lost to yield,
   Gave a quick glory to a desperate grace.

I saw him fall.   I saw the deadly stain
   Upon his breast — he cared not what was won.
The ghost was in the land of ghosts again.
   The curtain fell, the phantom play was done.

A WALL BETWEEN.

[A PITEOUS thing, you know,
Half hinted, at the edge of the earth, my friend.
　　Clinging to its last clod, She whispers low,
Not knowing that He has listened till the end.
　　A woman's tale (of wrong and grief),
　　And, therefore, none too brief.

　　He who could leave her heart,
Spite of youth's passionate promises, to break
　　(While through their children's home he walked, apart,
Dumb as the dead), must, for her soul's sweet sake,
　　Come, at the last, in priest-disguise
　　To help her to the skies !]

　　THEN, do I doubt ?　Not so.
Though the stars wander without any Guide
　　Out there in loneliest dark, almost I know
I do believe that He was crucified.
　　And risen and ascended to
　　The Heavens ?　Oh, priest, I do.

Still, you were kind to come.
Only to tell me, then, that I must die?
    I knew as much.   Ah me, the mouth was dumb
That told me first (let by-gone things go by), —
    The young sad mouth, without a breath.
    Yes, I believe in death.

    (A crucifix to kiss?)
Another world may light your lifted eyes,
    But, by my heart that breaks, I am of this.
Are you quite sure those palms of Paradise
    Do shelter for me one sweet head?
    Or, are the dead — the dead?

    It is a vain world?   Oh,
It is a goodly world, — a world wherein
    We hear the doves (that moan?) — the winds (that
      blow
The buds away?)   It is a world of sin,
    And therefore sorrow? — Was it, then,
    Fashioned and formed of men?

    Pray, would you give one rood
Of your dark, certain soil, where olives grow,
    For all those shining heights on heights, where brood

The wings you babble of that shame the snow?
——— Why, what new song?   But I have heard
In our own trees a bird.

(Oh, call it what you will !)
Light, hollow, brief, and bitter ?   Yes, I know.
With cruel seas and sands ? Yes, yes, and still ———
And fire and famine following where we go ?
And still I leave it at my feet,
Moaning, " The world is sweet."

Why, it was here that I
Had youth and all that only youth can bring.
Fair sir, if you would help a woman die,
Show me a glass.   There ! that one look will wring
My heart, I think, out of its place ; —
The earth may take my face.

Think of the blessèd skies ?
If in the cheek one have no rose to wear,
If nights all full of tears have changed the eyes, —
Why, would one be immortal and not fair ?
With faded hair, one would not quite
Contrast an aureole's light.

You talk of things unseen
With all the pretty arrogance of a boy.
    Why, one could laugh at what you think you mean.
You see the bud upon the bough with joy,
    You look through summer toward the fruit ———
    The worm is at the root?

    Well — if it is.   You see,
Your feet are set among our pleasant dews;
    Therefore, that crown of phantom stars for me,
In distance most divine, you kindly choose,
    Content to leave your own unwon,
    And shine here with the sun.

    Hush! Wait! Somehow — I know.
You do remind me tenderly of — yes,
    Of him, your kinsman (long, so long ago),
But for these sacred garments. I confess,
    Oh, father, I cannot forget
    The world where he stays yet!

    Quick! will you look away?
Too cruelly like him in the dusk you grow, —
    This awful dusk that ends it all, I say.

You pity us when we are young, you know,
    And lose a lover.   Surely then
    There may be other men.

    But when the hand we bind
So that it cannot reach out anywhere,
    Then find, or, sadder, fancy that we find,
The ring is not true gold, you do not care ; —
    These tragedies writ in wedding rings
    Are common, tiresome things.

    On earth there was one man, —
There were no men.   They all had faded through
    His shadow, Surely, where our grief began,
In that old garden, he, that one of two,
    Looked not to Eve before the Fall,
    So much the lord of all.

    And yet he said ——— I crave
Your patience.   I will not forget to die.
    And there is no remembrance in the grave ;
That comforts one.   Better it is to lie
    Not knowing thistles grow above,
    Than to remember love.

. . . . Now you may call my friends, —
Ah, my sweet friends.   They whispered just a word
    Or two last night here by me.   To what ends
They look through tears !   I thank them that I heard.
    " A charming chance," one lightly said ;
      The other's cheek burned red.

    The blush I could not see
I felt, like fire.   Then they both laughed, — and this
    Beside the dying.   He, they said, would be
Handsome and lonely.   Lonely ?   Will he miss
    The flower they bury in my breast,
      Up here with all the rest ?

    Yes, we have many a year,
And then we have one hour — and he away !
    Why, there was something only he should hear.
. . . . He wore his cloak ? — it is so cold for May.
    ——— If he would come (the lamp looks dim),
      I 'd leave the world — to him.

    Then tell him, priest, if he ———
Tell him, I pray you, this — ah, yet he said ———
    Then only tell him — nothing sweet for me.

Tell him I have not tasted once his bread
    Since then.   Tell him I die too proud
    To take of him a shroud.

    I, with the raven's trust
For food, the lily's trust for raiment, found
    Who feeds the one and clothes the other must
Remember me.   My hands, through many a wound,
    That which they had were glad to earn.
    He gave — what I 'll return.

    Ask him if I forgot
One household care. If I, in such poor ways
    As I could know, through piteous things have not
Tried still to please him, lo, these many days ; —
    Ah, bitter task, self-set and vain.
    ——— I hear the wind and rain.

    I fear he will be wet,
And — not afraid — but, somehow, something might
    Trouble him in the dark. You know he met
Strange men, somewhere, he said, one lonesome night.
    If anything should hurt him, I —
    Yes, I forgot — could die.

31

I have not seen his face
Since then.   We lived a wall apart, we two,
    While dark and void between us was all space.
Sometimes I hid, and watched his shadow through
        Too wistful eyes, as it would pass,
        Ghost-like, from off the grass.

Tell him, beneath his roof
I felt I had not where to lay my head,
    Yet could not dare the saintly world's reproof,
And withered under my own scorn instead ;
        Still whispering, " For the children's sake,"
        I let my slow heart break.

The children ?   Let them sleep —
To waken motherless.   Could I put by
    Their arms, and lie like snow, and have them weep,
With my own eyes so empty and so dry ?
        I 've left some pretty things, you see,
        To comfort them for me, —

Sweet dresses, curious toys ———
But, after all, what will the baby do ?
    . . . . Hush !   Here he is, waked by the wind's wild
        noise.

Let mamma count the dimples, one and two.
　　Whose baby has the goldest head?
　　I dreamed once he was dead.

　　Dead, and for many a year? —
Can a dead baby laugh and babble so?
　　Do you not see me kiss and kiss him here,
And hold death from me still to kiss him? — No?
　　Yet I did dream white blossoms grew ——
　　Do cruel dreams come true?

　　. . . . As the tree falls, one says,
So shall it lie.　It falls, remembering
　　The sun and stillness of its leaf-green days,
The moons it held, the nested bird's warm wing,
　　The promise of the buds it wore,
　　The fruit — it never bore.

　　So —— take my cross, and go.
Where my Lord Christ descended I descend.
　　Shall I ascend like Him? — I do not know.
I loved the world; the world is at an end.
　　Therefore, I pray you, shut your book,
　　And take away that look.

That look — of his! You stay.
Then, say I loved him bitterly to the last!
    Who loves one sweetly loves not much, I say.
Love's blush by moonlight will fade out full fast.
    Love's lightning scar at least we keep.
    Now, let me — go to sleep.

    . . . . His voice, too, in disguise!
It is ———— in pity, no! Yes, it is *he!* —
    With tears of memory in his steadfast eyes.
Mock-priest, how sharply you have shriven me!
    Your cousin's righteous robes ———— I fear
    You had somewhat to hear.

    Ah? —— Had you said but this
A year ago. Now, let my chill hand fall;
    It gives you back your youth. — But you will miss
My shadow from your sunshine. That is all.
    Yet — if some lovelier life shall dawn
    And I should love you on?

    Good-by. Was it well done?
You know that Eastern tale, where gifts of gold
    And glory — as a king's comfort — came to one
34

Who, having starved, went out with courtesy cold
   To meet and waive that bitter state,
   Dumbly, through his own gate.

TRANSFIGURED.

Almost afraid they led her in
   (A dwarf more piteous none could find) ;
Withered as some weird leaf, and thin,
   The woman was — and wan and blind.

Into his mirror with a smile —
   Not vain to be so fair, but glad —
The South-born painter looked the while,
   With eyes than Christ's alone less sad.

" Mother of God," in pale surprise
   He whispered, " What am I to paint! "
A voice, that sounded from the skies,
   Said to him : " Raphael, a saint."

She sat before him in the sun :
   He scarce could look at her, and she
Was still and silent. . . . . . " It is done,"
   He said, — " Oh, call the world to see ! "

Ah, this was she in veriest truth —
   Transcendant face and haloed hair.
The beauty of divinest youth,
   Divinely beautiful, was there.

Herself into her picture passed —
   Herself and not her poor disguise,
Made up of time and dust. . . . . At last
   One saw her with the Master's eyes.

FROM TWO WINDOWS.

HE was young — and he saw the South:
  The bird and the rose were there,
And the god with the lifted look
  And the laurel in his hair.
Before him a palace stood; —
  A shy wind moved the lace,
And showed by the light of a dream
  A woman's wonderful face.

He was old — and he saw the North:
  The mountains were fierce and bare,
And pitiless swords of ice
  Were thrust at him from the air.
A ruin blackened the moon;
  And in that forlornest place,
Wasted with famine and tears,
  Lo, a woman's dreadful face!

GOOD–BY.

[A WOMAN'S SONG.]

GOOD-BY, if it please you, sir, good-by.
This is a world where the wild-swans fly.
This is a world where the thorn hangs on
When the rose, its twin, is gone, is gone.
    Good-by — good-by — good-by.

Good-by, if it please you, sir, good-by.
You are here and away — I care not why.
This is a world where a man has his will,
A world where a woman had best be still.
    Good-by — good-by — good-by.

Good-by, if it please you, sir, good-by.
This is a world where — we see the sky;
After a while the stars will fall,
And the end will — make an end of it all !
    Good-by — good-by — good-by.

JEALOUS OF A STATUE.

YES, man her lover looks and dies,
    Wounded with her divine disdain ;
Then from his ashes seems to rise,
    Still young — to look at her again !

Sweet sir, I wonder not you sigh
    Her praise with all your little breath —
She must have time to listen.   I
    Make haste to keep my tryst with Death.

40

A LESSON IN A PICTURE.

So it is whispered here and there,
   That you are rather pretty?   Well?
(Here 's matter for a bird of the air
   To drop down from the dusk and tell.)
Let 's have no lights, my child.   Somehow,
The shadow suits your blushes now.

The blonde young man who called to-day
   (He only rang to leave a book? —
Yes, and a flower or two, I say!)
   Was handsome, look you.   Will you look?
You did not know his eyes were fine? —
You did not?   Can you look in mine?

What is it in this picture here,
   That you should suddenly watch it so?
A maiden leaning, half in fear,
   From her far casement; and, below,
In cap and plumes (or cap and bells?)
Some fairy tale her lover tells.

41

Suppose this lonesome night could be
  Some night a thousand springs ago,
Dim round that tower ; and you were she,
  And your shy friend her lover (Oh !)
And I — her mother !   And suppose
I knew just why she wore that rose.

Do you think I 'd kiss my girl, and say :
  " Make haste to bid the wedding guest,
And make the wedding garment gay, —
  You could not find in East or West
So brave a bridegroom ; I rejoice
That you have made so sweet a choice " ?

Or say, " To look forever fair,
  Just keep this turret moonlight wound
About your face ; stay in mid-air ; —
  Rope-ladders lead one to the ground,
Where all things take the touch of tears,
And nothing lasts a thousand years " ?

COUNSEL.

[IN THE SOUTH.]

My boy, not of your will nor mine
   You keep the mountain path and wait,
Restless, for evil gold to shine
   And hold you to your fate.

A stronger Hand than yours gave you
   The lawless sword.   You know not why.
That you must live is all too true,
   And — other men must die.

My boy, be brigand, if you must.
   But face the traveller in his track ;
Stand one to one, — and never thrust
   The dagger in his back.

Nay, make no ambush of the dark.
   Look straight into your victim's eyes,
Then — let his free soul, like a lark,
   Fly, singing, toward the skies !

43

. . . . My boy, if Christ must be betrayed,
　　And you must the betrayer be,
Oh, marked before the worlds were made !
　　What help is there for me ?

Ah, tell the prophets in their graves,
　　Who ask of you such blood as this,
" I take Him, then, with swords and staves,
　　I will not with a kiss ! "

44

A TRAGEDY IN WESTERN WOODS.

[WOMAN SPEAKS.]

WHY, we are willing, friend, to end with death;
　　Death to begin with is another thing.
Too bitter is it, not to keep our breath
　　Until its beat from this brave world we wring.

Confronting dew and briar-rose, pitiless sun,
　　And bird that sang not knowing, on her breast
A bud unwithered, damp with blood, lay one
　　Who dreamed of life, perhaps — and knew the rest.

The girl's shy lover, through weird, whispering trees
　　Walked eagerly, perhaps an instant late;
(That day of all days, feverish to please!)
　　He started, stared, and fell against the gate.

Blossom and blush he came to find.　He found
　　Only the dead — who left an empty earth.
—— But, sir, a ploughman's heart can hold a wound
　　As deep as if he cared for books or birth.

45

With tears unfallen, from out the murmurous crowd
    A woman trembled, who was sad and gray.
Lifting the maid she dressed her in her shroud,
    And watched her a long, still, wordless way.

"That boy!" one moaned; "why that could never be."
    Another said: "He owns what he has done."
She was a widow. As they muttered she
    Looked from the door — and saw her only son!

. . . . Ah, baby laugh and dimple, baby kiss
    And wandering baby hands, that take one's heart
To play with — or let drop and break! Was this
    The end, poor mother, of a mother's part?

We cry for help. God has the heavens to hold.
    Can He let fall the stars to take us up
And comfort us? He lets our lips grow cold —
    And that is much — after we drink the cup.

And she who saw men lead away that youth
    (The childish gold scarce blown from off his hair, —
More evil for his beauty's sake), in truth
    Saw no more sorrow, surely, anywhere!

If light come ever to the void in eyes
    That, having seen such woe, shut and are sealed,
It is the utter light of Paradise,
    Whereby no thing not fair shall be revealed.

AFTER THE QUARREL.

Hush, my pretty one.   Not yet.
   Wait a little, only wait.
Other blue flowers are as wet
   As your eyes, outside the gate
He has shut forever. — But
Is the gate forever shut?

Just a young man in the rain
   Saying (the last time?) " good-night ! "
Should he never come again
   Would the world be ended quite?
Where would all these rose-buds go? —
All these robins?   Do you know?

But — he will not come?   Why, then,
   Is no other within call?
There are men, and men, and men —
   And these men are brothers all!
Each sweet fault of his you 'll find
Just as sweet in all his kind.

None with eyes like his?   Oh — oh !
   In diviner ones did I

48

Look, perhaps, an hour ago,
   Whose?   Indeed (you must not cry)
Those I thought of — are not free
To laugh down your tears, you see.

Voice like his was never heard?
   No — but better ones, I vow;
Did you ever hear a bird? —
   Listen, one is singing now!
And his gloves?   His gloves?   Ah, well,
There are gloves like his to sell.

At the play to-night you 'll see,
   In mock-velvet cloaks, mock earls
With mock-jewelled swords, that he
   Were a clown by!   Now, those curls
Are the barber's pride, I say;
Do not cry for them, I pray.

If no one should love you?   Why,
   You can love some other still:
Philip Sidney, Shakespeare, ay,
   Good King Arthur, if you will;
Raphael — *he* was handsome too.
Love them one and all.   I do.

SAD SPRING–SONG.

BLUSH and blow, blush and blow,
   Wind and wild-rose, if you will;
You are sweet enough, I know —
You are sweet enough, but, oh,
Lying lonely, lying low,
   There is something sweeter still.

Come and go, come and go,
   Suns of morning, moons of night;
You are fair enough, I know —
You are fair enough, but oh,
Hidden darkly, hidden low,
   Lies the light that gave you light.

50

THE HOUSE BELOW THE HILL.

You ask me of the farthest star,
  Whither your thought can climb at will,
Forever questioning child of mine.
I fear it is not half so far
  As is the house below the hill,
Where one poor lamp begins to shine, —
The lamp that is of death the sign.

Has it indeed been there for years,
  In rain and snow, with ruined roof
For God to look through, day and night,
At man's despair and woman's tears,
  While with myself I stood aloof,
As one by some enchanted right
Held high from any ghastly sight?

. . . . One of my children lightly said:
  " Oh nothing, (Why must we be still?)
Only the people have to cry
Because the woman's child is dead
  There in the house below the hill.

I wish that we could see it fly ; —
It has gold wings, and that is why ! "

Gold wings it has?   I only know
   What wasted little hands it had,
That reached to me for pity, but
Before I thought to give it — oh,
   On earth's last rose-bud, faint and sad,
Less cold than mine had been, they shut.
Sharper than steel some things should cut !

. . . . I thought the mother showed to me,
   With something of a noble scorn
(When morning mocked with bird and dew),
That brief and bitter courtesy
   Which awes us in the lowliest born.
Ah, soul, to thine own self be true ; —
God's eyes, grown human, look thee through !

" We need no help — we needed it.
   You have not come in time, and so
The women here did everything.
You did not know?   You did not know ! "
   I surely saw the dark brows knit.

— To let the living die for bread,
Then bring fair shrouds to hide the dead!

What time I cried with Rachel's cry,
 I wondered that I could not wring,
While sitting at the grave forlorn,
Compassion from yon alien sky,
 That knows not death nor anything
That troubles man of woman born,
Save that he wounded Christ with thorn.

My sorrow had the right to find
 Immortal pity? I could sit,
Not hearing at my very feet
The utter wailing of my kind,
 And dream my dream high over it!
O human heart! what need to beat,
If nothing save your own is sweet?

Ah me, that fluttering flower and leaf,
 That weird, wan moon and pitiless sun,
And my own shadow in the grass
Should hide from me this common grief!
 Was I not dust? What had I done?
In that fixed face, as in a glass,
I saw myself to judgment pass!

"AH, CHASMS AND CLIFFS OF SNOW!"

Ah, chasms and cliffs of snow!
Down the dim path so many feet have beaten,
  Need it be hard to go? —
From bitter bread, from fruit the frost has eaten,
  From bloom the rain has shaken,
  From wings — the winds have taken?

  A few gold grains of corn
To plant in that strange soil, some hill-bird's feather,
  A broken branch of thorn
From some dead tree where two have watched together, —
  These, for the heart's close keeping
  Through waking or through sleeping!

  One moans with homesick breath,
Here, for gray crag and cloud, where vales are sunny:
  What then, if, after death,
One thirst for water, having milk and honey? —
  Sweeter divine regretting
  Were than divine forgetting!

DENIED.

I.

IT may have been ——— Who knows, who knows?
 It was too dark for me to see.
The wind that spared this very rose
 Its few last leaves could hardly be
 Sadder of voice than he.

A foreign Prince here in disguise,
 Who asked a shelter from the rain.
(The country that he came from lies
 Above the clouds.) He asked in vain,
 And will not come again.

If I *had* known that it was He
 Who had not where to lay his head: —
" But my Lord Christ, it cannot be ;
 My guest-room has too white a bed
 For way-side dust," I had said.

55

II.

[THE MOTHER'S THOUGHT.]

IT was my own sweet child — the one
　　Whose baby mouth breathes at my breast.
(A fairer and a brighter, none
　　Save His own Mother ever prest
　　　　Into diviner rest.)

He had escaped my arms and strayed
　　Into the pitiless world that night.
With wounded feet and faith betrayed,
　　Charmed backward by a glimmer of light,
　　　　Almost he stood in sight.

Oh, I had let *him* ask in vain,
　　(Vague, lonesome, shadowy years ahead,)
My roof to hide him from the rain,
　　My lamp to comfort him, my bread,
　　　　Who came as from the dead!

LIFE AND DEATH.

If I had chosen, my tears had all been dews;
  I would have drawn a bird's or blossom's breath,
Nor outmoaned yonder dove. I did not choose —
  And here is Life for me, and there is Death.

Ay, here is Life.   Bloom for me, violet;
  Whisper me, Love, all things that are not true;
Sing, nightingale and lark, till I forget —
  For here is Life, and I have need of you.

So, there is Death.   Fade, violet, from the land;
  Cease from your singing, nightingale and lark;
Forsake me, Love, for I without your hand
  Can find my way more surely to the dark.

57

DOUBLE QUATRAINS.

I.

"WE WOMEN."

HEART-ACHE and heart-break — always that or this.
  Sometimes it rains just when the sun should shine;
Sometimes a glove or ribbon goes amiss;
  Sometimes, in youth, your lover should be mine.

Still madam frets at life, through pearls and lace
  (A breath can break her pale heart's measured beat),
And still demands the maid who paints her face
  Shall find the world forever smooth and sweet.

II.

WORD OF COUNSEL.

OTHERS will kiss you while your mouth is red.
  Beauty is brief. Of all the guests who come
While the lamp shines on flowers, and wine, and bread,
  In time of famine who will spare a crumb?

Therefore, oh, next to God, I pray you keep
   Yourself as your own friend, the tried, the true.
Sit your own watch — others will surely sleep.
   Weep your own tears.   Ask none to die with you.

III.

BROKEN PROMISE.

AFTER strange stars, inscrutable, on high;
   After strange seas beneath his floating feet;
After the glare in many a brooding eye, —
   I wonder if the cry of "Land" was sweet?

Or did the Atlantic gold, the Atlantic palm,
   The Atlantic bird and flower, seem poor, at best,
To the gray Admiral under sun and calm,
   After the passionate doubt and faith of quest?

IV.

"TO BE DEAD."

IF I should have void darkness in my eyes
   While there were violets in the sun to see;
If I should fail to hear my child's sweet cries,
   Or any bird's voice in our threshold tree;

If I should cease to answer love or wit:
   Blind, deaf, or dumb, how bitter each must be!
Blind, deaf, or dumb — I will not think of it!
   . . . Yet the night comes when I shall be all three.

V.

THE HAPPIER GIFT.

Divinest words that ever singer said
Would hardly lend your mouth a sweeter red;
Her aureole, even hers whose book you hold,
Could give your head no goldener charm of gold.

Ah me! you have the only gift on earth
That to a woman can be surely worth
Breathing the breath of life for.   Keep your place.
Even she had given her fame to have your face.

VI.

IN DOUBT.

Through dream and dusk a frightened whisper said:
" Lay down the world: the one you love is dead."
   In the near waters, without any cry
   I sank, therefore — glad, oh so glad, to die!

Far on the shore, with sun, and dove, and dew,
And apple-flowers, I suddenly saw you.
   Then — was it kind or cruel that the sea
   Held back my hands, and kissed and clung to me?

VII.

A LOOK INTO THE GRAVE.

I LOOK, through tears, into the dust to find
   What manner of rest man's only rest may be.
The darkness rises up and smites me blind.
   The darkness — is there nothing more to see?

Oh, after flood, and fire, and famine, and
   The hollow watches we are made to keep
In our forced marches over sea and land —
   I wish we had a sweeter place to sleep.

VIII.

ETIQUETTE.

In some old Spanish court there chanced to be
   No one whose office was to save the king
From death by fire. The king himself? Not he; —
   Could royal hands have done so mean a thing?

My boy, through life think how this king of Spain
  (Whose name none knows — and so you 'll not forget !)
Caught by his palace hearth-flames, not in vain
  To ashes burned — for sake of Etiquette !

IX.

SEPTEMBER.

SEND back these lonesome lights to Fairyland,
  Whose wingèd glimmer of gold lured childish feet,
Borrowed (with bud and bird), you understand,
  To keep while moons were warm and dews were sweet,

Hush, — we may have them for a little yet
  Before the weird leaf-gathering frost creeps on.
Ah, loveliest time ! — wherein we may regret
  The fair things going, not the sweet things gone.

X.

FOR ANOTHER'S SAKE.

SWEET, sweet ? My child, some sweeter word than sweet,
  Some lovelier word than love, I want for you.
Who says the world is bitter, while your feet
  Are left among the lilies and the dew ?

. . . . Ah?   So some other has, this night, to fold
　　Such hands as his, and drop some precious head
From off her breast as full of baby-gold?
　　I, for her grief, will not be comforted.

WITH CHILDREN.

THE STORY OF LITTLE HENRY.

[AN INCIDENT FROM THE NEWSPAPER.]

YES, brown and rosy, perhaps, like you,
    Was the little child they have not found;
Or perhaps his eyes, like yours, were blue,
And his poor, sweet head faint-golden too —
    The little child who was drowned.

I hardly think his mother was right —
    Did she have it? — not to give him the bread;
But he shut the door, and then — " Good night;
(Yes, he went alone, and without any light "),
    " I 'll never come home," he said.

Poor little child, he was seven years old.
    Why, the bird's wild nest was new in the tree;
There were roses enough for him to hold
In his two small hands. —— But the river is cold
    In the summer-time, you see.

From the trouble of tears where did he go ? —
  Where did he go with his two bare feet ?
That life was bitter he seemed to know,
(What manner of bread did he think to eat ?) —
  Did he know that death was sweet ?

THE BABY'S BROTHER.

The Baby is brought for the lady to see;
" Was ever a lily-bud nicer than he ? "
But the door opens fiercely on cooing and kiss,
And — what merry outlaw from the greenwood is this ?

His brother ? — who laughs at himself in my face :
This picturesque vagabond, graceless with grace,
Whose head, like a king's come to grief, is discrowned ——
Ah, the kitten was wicked, and so she is drowned ?

All flushed with the butterfly chase, how he stands,
With a nestful of birds in his pitiless hands,
Which he mildly assures me were torn from the tree,
Or they 'd trouble their mother as Baby does me !

" Well, if Baby *is* sweet, you must love him right fast,
Because —— don't you know ?   Why, because he 'll not
        last!
For I was a baby, too, some of these days,
And just look at me *now !* " he unsparingly says.

TWO VOICES.

"ONE bird is come. It's blue. But there is not any
      other
  In this whole world anywhere, and it will soon be gone.
Will you listen?" "I must hush your pretty crying
      brother.
  Tell it — to sing on."

"Here's one rose, the first of all. But the wind may
      blow and take it,
  Or the frost may come again as cold as frost can be,
Or a bee that hunts for honey may light on the leaves
      and break it.
  Will you come and see?"

"Look on the floor, my boy, and think of my distresses :
  Aladdin's lamp (upset) and Blue Beard's dreadful key,
The Sleeping Beauty's coverlet and Cinderella's dresses,
  Full of dust — ah, me!"

"Now a star is out. It 's gold. But I tell you it will
never
Look so shining any more where the water is so deep."
" Oh, the star will stay, I fancy, somewhere in the sky
forever ;
I — must go to sleep.

. . . . "It will stay. But I shall stay not. Why was I
sent hither,
Fair brief world, if I must leave you, having seen nor
heard
(Resting in your grass an instant on my secret mission —
whither ?)
Star, nor bloom, nor bird ?

" I *would* help you find the fairies (for the *moon* can shine
on pleasure),
I would hear the bird a-singing, I would see the rose
was red,
If I only had a little of the long, long leisure
I shall have — when dead."

THE QUEEN OF SPAIN.

Ah, then she was a bride, a king's bride, too
    (With crimson velvet mantles lit with gold),
And beautiful? Those fairy-tales are true
    That end in sorrow, somewhere we are told.
And so you envied her? Tell me, I pray,
    How fares the Queen of Spain to-day?

Oh, now you only pity her? I see.
    Almost with tears you pity her — and why?
Death is the saddest thing of all — and she
    Is dead? Therefore — she will not have to die;
Nor have to live, for life itself may prove
    Not quite too sweet, for all of love.

You envied her what time the priest who bent
    To bless the bridal might have seen in air
His own ghost holding the Last Sacrament
    To her loth lips, and weirdly waiting there.
They hunger not who taste that pleasant bread.
    . . . . Poor child, what is it to be dead?

72

Oh, some who envied not her pearls and trains,
  Her Spanish lover and her Spanish crown,
Do envy her the one thing that remains
  To those who keep their hollow hands shut down ;
For whether that one thing in truth be rest,
  Or Paradise, it is the best.

1873.

THE HAPPIEST MAN.

[TOLD TO A LITTLE BOY.]

WELL, when the moon and stars were new
The richest king of all took up
A rose, and shook a drop of dew
Into a rather precious cup
Worth — shall I say a world or two?

" Take this," that richest king began
To tell his prettiest page, " my boy,
And find the owner as you can.
Follow the wind.   I wish you joy."
The inscription read : " The Happiest Man."

The prettiest page went here and there.
His silken suits did fade with rain,
Sea-mist uncurled his lovely hair ;
He questioned torrid stars in vain ; —
The Cup grew heavier in his care.

74

At last a dim, weird hut he found ;
The ice flashed sharp on every thorn ;
The lost leaves made a withering sound ;
 Grim shadows crouched in rocks forlorn ;
No blossom breathed for miles around.

Through one low window one low light
Showed two poor graves a step apart :
One prisoned safely, out of sight,
A boy who broke his mother's heart ;
One sheltered her from snow and night.

A man not old, but gray and thin,
Half starved, half frozen, dying slow,
In whose deep eyes the tears had been
Too often — and too long ago —
Moaned him a welcome from within.

"This world that, somehow, seems to be
 A wretched place, holds none, I know,
So wretched on the whole as he :
Therefore I 'll leave my Cup and go ; "
So thought the prettiest page, you see.

The stranger sighed : " Why leave it here ?
Go take it to the Happiest Man."
" Oh, you are he.   I 'll make it clear,"
The prettiest page replied : " I can.
For you are — the most wretched, sir.

" Hunger and cold and loneliness,
And something more, are in your looks,
Some sorrow words could not confess.
These things (as I have read in books),
Make people happy, sir, I guess."

" They have not made me happy.
Am made of dust and not of ink.
Youth, love, and gold enough to buy
Him bread, the man must have, I think,
Whose wine shall flush your Cup.   Good-by."

Back to the richest king, I say,
The prettiest page went sad with doubt.
It was the royal wedding day :
Soldiers and priests came glittering out.
He stood and watched the fountains play.

76

He dreamed awake, while many a band
With bridal marches charmed the air ;
And still the Cup was in his hand.
The young, sweet queen, who saw it there,
Wondered thereat, I understand.

The prettiest page here hung his head —
" Alack, what was my travel worth ?
I 've had — a wild-goose chase," he said ;
" There is no Happiest Man on earth.
I rather think he must be dead."

" ' To the Happiest Man,' " so read the queen,
Then blushed and blushed like anything ;
(She was a bride, that 's all I mean.)
" Pray take it to my lord, the king ;
He 'll drink from it to-day, I ween."

The prettiest page stared with surprise —
" Madam, my lord, the king, you know,
Has golden hair and splendid eyes,
And vales of bloom and cliffs of snow,
And nightingales and butterflies.

," He, if our gray-beard seers speak true,
    Was born beneath the kindliest star
    In all the heavens.   (I guess they knew.)
    Leisure and pleasure, peace and war,
    He has, and, Madam, he has — you.

" Therefore he 's wretched (for these things
    Make people happy), on my word.
    No one has headache like these kings,
    Or heartaches like these queens, I 've heard."
    . . . . There, listen how that blue-bird sings !

Why did he shake the drop of dew
    Out of the rose?   Oh, you may guess ;
    I never read his " Reasons " through,
    For this quaint action, I confess.
    Who. had the Cup ?   Well — guess that, too.

TWO AND TWO.

A BROWN head and a golden head
 Above the violets keep in sight;
Dark eyes and blue (with tears to shed)
 Look laughing toward me in the light.
A red-bird flashes from the tree:
" The world is glad, is glad!" sings he.

A golden head, a head of brown,
 Below the violets, miss the sun;
Dark eyes and blue — their lids shut down —
 With tears (and theirs were brief) have done.
A dove hides in another tree:
" The world is sad, is sad!" grieves she.

Through song and moan, I hardly know,
 Between the red-bird and the dove,
If most I'd wish that two below
 The violets were with two above,
Or two above the violets lay
With two below them deep, to-day.

FROM NORTH AND SOUTH.

[A LESSON FROM THE NEWSPAPER.[1]]

" SOME people have the loveliest time.
    I 'm tired of learning everything ! "
" You have not learned it yet. We climb
     Great mountains slowly, child, and bring
  Few flowers into the huts below,
  When down for bread and sleep we go." ·

 " Just read this letter. Oh, how sweet
     She must have looked ; — only one year
  Older than I, too." " Very neat
     Her hat and plume may be, my dear."
" ' More queenly than a queen ' " — " Just so "
" ' In her dark purple habit.' " — (" Oh ! ")

" ' Then at the ball that night she wore
    Only one blush-rose in her hair

1 September, 1878.

And one in either cheek.'" — "What more
  Needs any charming Miss to wear?
They do not cost like lace and pearls,
  You saddest of gold-headed girls."

"That's from the North."   "Now turn and read
  A letter from the South, I say."
"'Nothing but Death is here'" — "Indeed?"
"'And Misery following Death.'"   "Ah me! —
  That's of some people, too, you see."

6   81

ONE YEAR OLD.

So, now he has seen the sun and the moon,
  The flower and the falling leaf on the tree
(Ah, the world is a picture that's looked at soon),
  Is there anything more to see?

He has learned (let me kiss from his eyes that tear),
  As the children tell me, to creep and to fall; —
Then life is a lesson that's taught in a year,
  For the baby knows it all.

CHILD'S-FAITH.

These beautiful tales, I trust, are true.
　　But here is a grave in the moss,
And there is the sky.　And the buds are blue,
　　And a butterfly blows across.

Yes, here is the grave and there is the sky; —
　　To the one or the other we go.
And between them wavers the butterfly,
　　Like a soul that does not know,

Somewhere?　Nowhere?　Too-golden head,
　　And lips that I miss and miss,
You would tell me the secret of the dead —
　　Could I find you with a kiss!

. . . . Come here, I say, little child of mine,
　　Come with your bloom and breath.
(If he should believe in the life divine,
　　I will not believe in death!)

" Where is your brother ? " — I question low,
    And wait for his wise reply.
Does he say, " Down there in the grave ? " Ah, no ; —
    He says, with a laugh, " In the sky ! "

EVERYTHING.

[A FAIRY TALE.]

You 'd call his room a pleasant place :
Satin and rose-wood, lights and lace,
And fruits and vines were there.   (Ah, well.)
And yet the rich man rang his bell,
When lo, he saw a fairy flit
From outside dusk to answer it.

Her flower-like eyes, so faint and blue,
Looked at him through her veil of dew ;
Though every gracious thing he had,
His face was fretful, tired, and sad : —
"Pray, sir," she whispered, "did you ring ?"
He said : "Yes, I want — everything !"

The fairy laughed and walked away.
Ragged and rosy at his play,
A boy who had the grass, the dew,
Birds, bees, the sun, the stars, like you,
She met : "What do you want ?" sighed she.
"Oh ! I have everything," said he.

FORGIVENESS.

Go show the bee that stung your hand,
The sweetest flower in all the land;

Then, from its bosom, she will bring
The honey that will cure the sting.

86

DOUBTFUL COMPLIMENT.

" Oh, mamma," sobbed the troubled little maid,"
    " Please tell me, will you, that it is not true ;
It breaks my heart : that hateful Rose, she said —
    Just think of it ! — she said I looked like you !"

THE SIGHT OF TROUBLE.

So, then, my boy, you want to know
    Just what is trouble? Some great day, no doubt,
When all this world is full of rain or snow,
Or lonesomer because the birds sing so;
Or some strange night, when this same moon drops low
    On many graves — or one — you will find out.

.You do not want to wait, I fear —
    You want to see it now, or pretty soon?
The woman dressed in black so who was here
Said she saw trouble always? It *is* queer
That she sees things you cannot see, my dear.
    ———— Did I say there was trouble in the moon?

No, but I think it may be there,
    For people see it when they lie awake.

And in the sun as well, and in the air,
And in the tangles of some yellow hair,
And in the wind that blows it everywhere —
    Except to Heaven (if I do not mistake).

Once when her boy was dead, ah, me !
    It would not let her sleep? ———— Is it a ghost?
Why, if it were a ghost, then it would be
Something, or nothing, that we cannot see !
And yet it is a ghost, sometimes, and we
    Just think we see it, in the dark, at most.

Do women, then, wear glasses so
    They can see trouble?   Hardly, I'm afraid ;
Perhaps they see it plainer with them, though.
Oh, as to men !   Indeed, I do not know.
They miss the train because their watch is slow,
    And drink such coffee as was never made ;

They have to wait till some one brings
    Their hat and gloves and overcoat and all,
After that terrible last church-bell rings,
While she is only doing fifty things
Between the tying of her bonnet-strings,
    The baby's cries, and putting on her shawl.

So these poor men see trouble too,
   In their own way, a little, I suppose.
Still, what is trouble? Just see here, if you
Tore off that first white rose before I knew
How sweet it was, and cut this lace all through,
   Too well I know how well your mother knows.

A HINT FROM HOMER.[1]

I LET the sun stand still, this lonesome day,
   And hardly heard the very baby coo,
(Meanwhile the world went on — the other way!)
   That I might watch the siege of Troy with you.

The great Achilles (whom we knew) was there —
   His shining shield was what we knew him by;
And Hector with his plume of horse's hair
   Frightened his child and laughed to hear it cry.

Poor Hector! Never sorrow for the dead,
   In these three thousand rather piteous years,
Stole into sweeter words than Helen said
   Beside him, through the dropping of her tears.

We grieved with Priam for his gracious son.
   Much-wandering Ulysses with his craft
Cheated us through strange seas — and every one
   Came straight to grief with him upon his raft.

[1] *Stories from Homer*, by Rev. Alfred J. Church.

A HINT FROM HOMER.

Not one among you but could draw his bow,
    After its rest in Ithaca, and bring
A suitor down ! — In the dark backward, oh,
    How sad the swallow-twitter of its string !

Now, that it's time to shut the shadowy book,
    (Ah me, they clash together, left and right,
And Greek meets Greek — or Trojan ! Only look !) —
    What have you learned from it ? You say : " To
        fight ! "

MY LITTLE FLOWER–BOY.

" Here are more and more, and here are ever so many,"
　　Dimpled and brown and breathless, he hurries to me to
　　　　say :
" This is the reddest of all and this is the bluest of any
　　I have brought you every one there was in the world
　　　　this day."

Yes, they *are* sweet, so sweet that each by itself is better
　　Than the grains of gold in the sands or the seeds of
　　　　pearl in the sea ;
So sweet that you could n't spell how sweet with every
　　　　letter
　　In Shakespeare's book, nor write how sweet if you
　　　　were as great as he.

But flowers, and flowers, and flowers, all crowded and
　　　　crushed together,
　　They tire one just a little, if they *are* pretty, you
　　　　know ; —

The earth has nothing to do but blossom, this indolent
    weather.

You may take them all away — and bring me one
    when there's snow.

LITTLE CHRISTIAN'S TROUBLE.

His wet cheeks looked as they had worn,
  Each, with its rose, a thorn,

Set there (my boy, you understand?)
  By his own brother's hand:

"Look at my cheek. What shall I do? —
  You know I have but two!"

His mother answered, as she read
  What my Lord Christ had said,

(While tears began to drop like rain :)
  "Go, turn the two again."

95

MIDSUMMER–NIGHT FAIRIES.

(THE FIREFLIES.)

LET 's see.   We believe in wings,
　　We believe in the grass and dew,
We believe in the moon — and other things
　　That may be true.

But are there any ?   Talk low ;
　　(Look ! what is that eery spark ?)
If there *are* any, why, there they go,
　　Out in the dark !

www.ingramcontent.com/pod-product-compliance
Lightning Source LLC
Chambersburg PA
CBHW020031030726
47499CB00007B/2372